an island of fifty

Ben Brooks

[mud luscious press]

first printing: 2010

cover design: Steven Seighman

editor: J. A. Tyler

associate editor: Andrew Borgstrom

online: www.mudlusciouspress.com

acknowledgments

Thanks to Jim & Carah, who read this first & said kind things about it.

Thanks to J. A. Tyler for his hard work.

Thanks to whoever's reading this.

an island of fifty

Ben Brooks

t r e e s

> *Maps: I, II*
> *Noise*
> *Day*
> *Fuchsia*
> *Plague: I, II, III, IV, V*
> *Tunnels: I, II, III, IV, V*
> *Scabs: I, II, III, IV, V, VI, VII, VIII, IX, X*
> *Justice: I, II, III, IV, V, VI*
> *Hymns: I, II, III*
> *Poppies: I, II, III, IV*
> *Shou Sui: I, II, III, IV*

s a i n t s

> *Hunger: I, II, III, IV, V*
> *Heart: I, II, III, IV*
> *Lights: I, II, III, IV, V, VI, VII*
> *Sun: I, II, III*
> *Men*
> *Lessons: I, II*
> *Union*
> *Disease: I, II, III*

f l o o d s

t r e e s

PREMISE ONE:

Civilization is not & can never be sustainable. This is especially true for industrial civilization.

Endgame Vol. 1, The Problem of Civilization : Derrick Jensen

m a p s

I

Marsha lays paths & **tears them up**.

The mill is in sight.

Eyes are wretched chunks of light.

I carry in my palms her heart
& it throbs with the pulse of a lion. She
drinks oxblood on the island. There is
a mill on the island. I am weary but my
feet pulse with the throb of a chariot:
ONWARD.

Marsha talks of beauty with the
Hotelier. He is African-American. Watch his
gargantuan jaw swell with words.

They stand beside the marble monolith,
beside the mill, beside the chariot, beneath the

charioteer.

The charioteer, the hotelier claims, breathes saffron & lives within the trunk of a great oak. He bites into the claws of crabs & washes taste away with woodbines. He pays for cold coffee-skinned girls from the ships to gyrate against his spine.

Marsha feigns horror & lifts her skirt. She draws the cross over her breast. The blades of the mill begin to show cracks & the orphans grow restless. People are checking out. There is a small man in the mill who spins thread & bloodies his wrinkled fingers.

One day they will fold, his mother says.

Let them die, he tells her.

The Hotelier lights torches &

shrieks. He has struck **silver brass copper gold**; we can mould an industrial civilization he screams. The charioteer pauses. Horses urinate into pockets of poppies.

No bother, he says, all civilization will water into streams.

No. You don't understand. You understand nothing. You kiss your Pegasus & I will flourish.

maps

II

She sets fires for the forests that bloom.

Sweet Acacia watches the island from her island.

My island, she sings songs from the black book. A book of ten curves, a sky, an unplotted trajectory.

Cradling a copper shotgun in the hem of her pinafore, **she sips liquid gold** from a wooden flask.

Acacia, I see them. I watch their bodies sway in the solar wind. **Beautiful frames** of bone, stretch the skin over & paint them with ochre. Red ochre from Arnhem. A bird with the spirit of a man. He perches on my wrist & caws declarations of an apocalypse, unrequited love, the discovery of bastard minerals. My ears are small & choked with wax.

They have discovered silver on the island, Acacia.

Uncloak your head.
She narrows green eyes to scarlet keyholes & barks orders to her body through a thousand nerve routes. They splinter. They are a thousand. They are led.

Blowing sharp oil fine over the moths.
They will glow white hot on our hands this evening, Acacia.

We will send them to the island quarry. We will not dream.

They have

struck industrial civilization.

Stop them before it is too late. Teach them to build walls around their lusts. Teach them it is impossible to pocket cloud.

Crush the tendons in their hands to spices!

Flavor the stained lambs & throw them to waves.

Acacia, we sung the moths' hymns until the mother boxed our ears & took them on her shoulders. She wandered through the night like a biblical drunk.

Swallowing dream.

White sheet over thin body.

I watched her. I saw. My eyes caging.

Her eyes are on the island.
Industrial civilization. I see ethereal shapes rising.

I see hypothetical statues of peasants clutching hypothetical statuettes of industrial giants.

Island minds impregnated with wild dreams of green paper stacks & worship. I hear their dreams murmur numbers into white ears.

They want to know, Acacia. They want maps.

The charioteer chases thoughts of avarice into the clouds & cries inside the hollow of a sycamore. I see woodbine smoke gulp from the ends of branches.

Give up give up give up give up give up give up give up give up give up.

I feel the hot wire of a wooden cage. He sleeps beneath the wings of sparrows, hawks pick them off as metals emerge from the rocks.

I watch Marsha spin hearts on bare earth. She plucks vegetables & muddies her sweet symmetry.

We will need more, she says.
& they send for bricks from the ocean.

n o i s e

Paris welcomes ships into the dock he has shaped with rock & scarred hands. Even sky curls at change. Our hands are small but we have minds.

This is the start of industrial civilization, he says. Paris is a quiverer.

They have sent for red bricks to build red brick houses. Nuclear families will live out textbook dreams.

The island has a cathedral now, the island has steam.

The Miller bleeds tears over his frayed knots. He thinks of the gold & hunts for amber among the branches of a sweet chestnut.

This is a revolution for the young, bent priest of dead arcadia.

It is a fuchsia night & a scarlet morning will follow.

He collects wood, wire, & steaks from the Wagyu cattle. Tobacco smoke hardens tears to resolve in the dark of the mill.

Paris claps a captain's back & whistles for the Charioteer. The Charioteer (& he shall be known as Hector) shook birds from his hair & eyed the new stone with suspicion. He gripped the reigns of his horses like a mother as the crew talked riot behind his mind. Paris beams at a richer future. Hector slaps his thighs. Paris, what can you not see? Whispers turn wheels;

& the Hotelier sent smoke into the sky! The Miller saw smoke &

cried into his hands. He thought of his wife & ran cotton around his arms until they turned white without blood. He felt the red water soar into his head & a hot melancholy overwhelmed him. The crew arrives at the renamed NEW STATE HOTEL & flicks flecks of gold at the sleeping Hotelier. In marble chambers they drink themselves apart with vodka. To a new world, they cheer.

They dance. They will go to find greater lands than this, clutching at nothing but slim hopes & solemn bottles. From birth they heard the motors & heralded the gold. In dull light they fall over each other. The Hotelier sighs & picks gold flecks from the carpet.

These are roots.

Hotelier

Does gold feel warm?
I believe in gold, yes.

Mirrors?
The sailors leave tales & tales carry the young like fire. Fire cannot break bone. Fire can melt skin.

Ready?
I will embrace the new world with fists. I want for gold & marble. The marble palace, they will say. Blow smoke rings into the ceiling & lick your lips. I am going to be a rich man, watch my chest expand; there is a white dream inside of my ribcage. Am I beautiful?

& at night?
No, not any more. Why want with such an exquisitely brazen light beside your heart? No, I can crush flies with my fingers but this is more, this is an ocean. Labor & war.

d a y

Marsha boils potato for her Uncle & smokes his dark tobacco. The house smells of beeswax & mud.

A scarlet morning will soon eat this; wooden shack lying on the line between village & forest. Everything is gone.

I fire her dress to hear her laughter. She has the most rapturous laugh. It grips my arms & blows streams of sweet jasmine through my ears. The Miller spins cotton & sings a song of timber. He hears Chariot wheels skim stones over the paths. We are an island of fifty, he sings.

The body of the charioteer's wife

watches the beams of their cottage bend.

He does not remember how she died.

Marsha spoons potato into her Uncle
& cries silently. She weeps prophetic
into his gray beard as he prays in
streams of thought.

Marsha wishes for white fire &
thick skin.

The Miller's mother laughs from beneath
her thin duvet, hysteria!

Moths sit white hot on the hands of The
Miller & he knows that it is time for
dream.

f u c h s i a

On the first of the fuchsia nights,
Hector does not run dreams.

He smokes woodbines but does not eat
& when the Milliner's son arrives with a
hatbox he breathes saffron so hard into
the boy's eager eyes that it turns to frost
& makes the child run.

The night turns red as he watches dreams descend tentative
from naked skies.

He remembers. He watches **avarice**
twist itself through the minds of
orphans sleeping in the basement of the

mill, he watches **majesty** slip through
the mouths of women in The Moon

& Earth, he watches **blindness**
tumble through the ears of men
drinking in mud shacks.

Hector drinks gin & slaps his head
against the corpse of his wife. He stokes
the fire.

He does not remember how she died.

The fire trips over itself. He cries for the
dreams he has not stopped. He prays to
his wife that the world will not collapse.
The Charioteer hears his horses whine
ash into the night & he cries for them.
He passes through to the stable & lies
in matted straw beside a chestnut mare.
The horse beats its hooves into the air;

a dream of chasing nothing through nowhere. Sorry, Hector says.

plague

I

In the scarlet morning
Marsha rakes dry earth & whistles
promises to the land. She listens for
the chariot trot & can hear nothing. The
charioteer sleeps with drunk
dreams in the hollow of his willow
tree while his mother screams prayers
into the sun.

She prays for gold & coal & steel,
her dreams have brought her lust & they
shake her rotting body to life.

Brown teeth are bared in excitement. Let
the ships sail, she howls, let them
bring us wealth. Still her son
sleeps with his dizzy dreams of forest.
He is one of the lucky few. Marsha sits alone

on the beach with her rake & watches
the waves. She drinks from a flask of
oxblood.

They bring fortunes from the east. She
curses them with spit & lights a pipe.
I will search out the source
of the dreams of Industrial
Civilization, she vows.

The waves murmur of discontent in
circles. They claw at her feet.

The Hotelier serves platters of fish &
potato to the visiting crew who laugh
saline spittle over his dishes. They toss
the platters of earth's food & call for
wine & veal. Industrial civilization, he
whispers, picking up shards of clay,
industrial civilization. He watches them
ink anchors on each other's thick arms &
he sighs. The hotel must be made. Marble
floors & broad staircases. Chandeliers.

There must be chandeliers, & tiled baths.
Copper taps will shine. & a safe, a
safe will be needed. Inches of steel will
keep me safe.

p l a g u e

I I

Red brick houses begin to replace mud
shacks as the village men mix cement,
topless in the scarlet sun. Their wives
gossip in the cathedral. They talk of
fortunes to be had & exotic fruits
to be found. The bishops paint their
crucifixes with gold & fix the spines of
bibles. The cathedral glows with the sweat
of men polishing its stone.

p l a g u e

I I I

The Miller burns his thread.
He hooks wire around the wood he has collected & then pins steak to the finished trap. They are set around the shack.

The industrial giants will not reach me, he says. Cradling his legs, The Miller calls for moths but they do not come. Scarlet morning shatters into white afternoon.

Marsha draws maps into the sand of the beach. LET THEM COME, The Miller screams. His mother beckons him to bed.

Pray with me, she bows her head.

Rain falls in vats.

Let us pray for gold to fill our mouths & choke us.

He runs from the house & falls into a trap. His thin leg bleeds sludge over the slice of steak.
Running blind.
Running wild.

Tripping wild into a cage. He runs for the forest, for the charioteer.

COME, he cries.

The charioteer climbs naked out of the tree trunk in drunken haze, a long cigarette hanging limp from his lips.

Give it up, he says, turning his back on The Miller, let them win.

FUCK. The Miller throws his weight

into a slap against Hector's cheek.
LOOK AT ME. The charioteer falls &
The Miller sits over his bare torso.

Theyarecoming&theywillkeepcom
ingwhilethedreamsdie&keepcomi
ng&keepbreakinggoodmindstobad
bentswithdrunkenpaintedportraits
ofhappinessiswealth.

Hector's glazed eyes. His eyes are wet.
Tear.

Please, The Miller says, I will run dreams with you.
He climbs off the man's body & they
sit side by side. We can't stop them, the
charioteer says. Shrug. We will run
dreams tonight. & EVERY NIGHT
AFTER THAT The Miller adds. &
every night until we are broken, Hector
says.

I make promises to Marsha & set her wet heart back inside her chest. I watch her leave. I look at her Uncle. It's just us now I say, laying wild garlic beneath his pillow.

The Miller

Them?
The young too fast to throw their nets. Hector tries, we ride, too far fuchsia. You see my knees? Fight violence with violence, I won that off a merchant in The Moon & Earth. I don't believe in the sharp metals.

The insides?
She screams yes. Dreams have lodged like chicken bones inside her throat. All she can do is scream & sleep. Watch her in the winter, she will drink it all down. Her lungs will sag below her feet.

The line?
A stream of oil between our feet perhaps.
A crack above our heads. The last tree
will spill soil over the water & the glass
words will be blown red before our eyes.
I believe in sky & grass.

In the days to come?

Smoke it down, drink it down,

make yourself vomit. Vomit over
polished bullion bars, take it back.

plague

IV

Acacia watches the island from her island. She polishes her shotgun & laughs at the drunk crew flailing on their moored boat. She sees it set sail & prays it sink while the men laugh hysterically.

Boats come daily. Drink liquid gold.

They bring red bricks & strange foods. Marsha does not sing from the beach any longer, she notices. The port has become hard gray lines. The ships have become steel faces tearing merciless slits in the ocean.

Bandage the sea. Bandage

everything.

Acacia picks vegetables, fruit, then smokes a cigarette & watches the sky burn confused. The sky sorrows. She can see that the people are growing restless in the greenhouse heat of growth. People want.

She remembers old time; Old town. She remembers farming, sweat with trade. She remembers the cobbler & The Miller drunk. She remembers Marsha skipping surf in mornings. She remembers naked flames. She remembers arms & women & wine & song & wood & scent & smile & dance & sparrows & moths & chariots & yellow days, black nights, open palms, the gift of silver, flat land, safe land, empty hotels & faces. She remembers people. She remembers people sweating, working under a plastic sun as willing slaves. She remembers love & not courtship. She remembers the absence of a cathedral. Man's phallus in God's young sky.

p l a g u e

V

The cathedral built from red bricks was
the first pike to tear the sky
above our island.

Paris conducted the men who snapped spines heaving blocks from the port around town in circles.

The bishops drank vodka & mocked the sins of workers.

Snares & lashes beat a rhythm even Acacia could hear. They sat back through crimson night, Paris & the bishops; they smiled at progress & thanked God for
all things high. All things
green cowered black beneath the new sky.

The charioteer cried heretical into his

hands & broke the branches from his Oak. The Miller whispered. Everyone whispered. People whispered equality, people whispered; its just the way things are. The workers' wives bleached their hair. They smoked menthol cigarettes & whispered. The whole town whispered their inhibitions to a sky that set late beneath the pin pricks of a thousand cigarettes.

The moths landed white on their hands but dreams did not come.

The dreams had been set. Acacia felt the burn of moths on her hands & on her arms & on her eyes. She dreamed for days.

She dreamed a crone smoking a cigarette & flicking the butt into a forest which blazed. Naked children ran laughing from between the trees. Acacia rolled in the ash plains left behind & then woke. When she woke a lamb was slaughtered & her copper shotgun polished. She eyed the islanders. They smoked & cast suspicion over her flasks of liquid gold. The cathedral shook.

t u n n e l s

I

Marsha grips her wet heart & faces the forest. Industrial civilization, she whispers.

The trees, unaware, dream, bark begins to peel.

There is a Lunatic who stalks badgers through the forest. His soles are hard & shot through with pine needles. Marsha whistles God's grievances & tidies the forest paths. She sweeps with bare hands & works tirelessly. As night penetrates the spaces between leaves she sleeps with a single moth in an abandoned badger set.

Marsha

Success?
The root of dreams of industrial

civilization will be a steel giant & I
will feed him my heart. This
town for my bundle of dreams. I will
never let them shoot needles through my
spine. Watch me.

From now?
I can throw rocks into the ocean.

Everything will live.

t u n n e l s

I I

A steel boat hits the harbor with pointed blue hull. History, she is called.

The islanders gather.
The charioteer sits in his Sycamore & watches men open their arms. An army of men in desert tan boilersuits file out of the ship & a giant in an olive drab woolsack proudly smokes beside them.

He turns to the townspeople. MINE, he says grinning. Streets of red brick houses form grids over the island. The hotelier grips his wife's hand.

They sweat. The town sweats. The town's sweat trickles into the ocean & the ocean layers with scum & the scum filters down the throats of swallows who fly in twisted circles, broken wings & drown. Brine welcomes flightless bodies

into its great cape. Oh great fold of salt &
muscle. Sinew stretches the skin of birds.

I think of beauty & they think of the beautiful.

The olive drab woolsack man
points fishbone fingers at distance.
Edges of the town; plains, hills.
This small scale coal riot. Desert tan
boilersuits quench a voyage lasting years
with watered down gin at the hotel.

The charioteer plots for a coup,
Acacia polishes pistols.

Paris admires olive drab woolsack man
& casts promises inside chicken wire
around the man's neck. You shall lead
this town from the dark ages, he says.
The Miller's ears blister. The woolsack
man nods. Send for more ships, red bricks & women.

t u n n e l s

I I I

The ships come. Hector drinks oxblood on the beach while they spit steel cages onto the island. He runs dreams each night with The Miller. There are almost none now, it is too late. **Misery morning smoke blue.** All of the dreams evaporate into the pores of leaves. Moths lie restless on the roofs of red brick houses. Hands grow cold in the evenings & people replay dreams from their night of hegemony. The night of hegemony was a beautiful end, Acacia.

I try to light moths with oil & matches but they project onto the sky & burn up in fuchsia atmosphere. Hector & The Miller light woodbines in the branches of a willow.

They survey the town; olive drab, desert

tan. Soon there will be fires. Fires & motors & men-devils. Thick set concrete chimneys sculpting clouds to police the populace. This is how it started & this is how it will end. They look at the men & say, this will do no good & the men look at the land & say, this will bring us wealth. More ships. They want more ships. The island cannot sustain itself now.

Dependence, The Miller whispers. Resources, Hector replies.

t u n n e l s

I V

Marsha is woken by the forest man
loudly licking lips beside her ears.
Licking the lips of a fox he caught mid-
howl with thick hands round its thin
neck. He wrestles her over a pathway

& into a hole. **A fire burns**. She
slips between dreamless sleep & the
underground chamber. The man roasts
fox over his fire & watches her breasts
rise & fall. For whole moments the man
sits happy. He presents her with fox
ribs & the two suck charred meat from
yellow bone on the floor of the room.

We live like kings, he says.
This fox will please gods.
Your town is a hole of suspicion now.

I will to find the roots of dreams.

The man laughs & his tongue curls back

on itself, inside a toothless cavity.
You search for avarice.
& where may I find him?
She. A girl. She lies with the wild dogs in a field of poppies.
Take me.
Take yourself.
You will have nothing here.
I notice myself grow older & laugh.

You will not laugh forever.
No.
There are lines that run through time.

Tork fee waye undoe soo tra.
You are wrong.
Marsha runs from the room through the hole above their heads. She smokes a cigarette on the forest floor & walks. She wills to find the root of dreams, industrial civilizations.

The Lunatic

People?

Floods will break their pristine red bricks & the shards will slice their sicksad bodies. They have no maps. Avarice strikes matches. They only want for more motors, the girl in the field told me that.

Me?

No, no, no, no nobody lives in the trees. Put down your flowers bear. You have good eyes, Your mother never told you? I'll tell you now. I will hold you too. We can live in a tree if you wish it. I will paint your body, you will like that.

You too?

That way, maybe; that way; here!

t u n n e l s

V

Hector & The Miller hitch horses to the chariot. Blank sky unfolds like a tarpaulin over them; they ride in circles. The town, devoid of dream, sleeps silent without the moths. Moths climb red brick rooftops & tumble to cinder deaths at the foot of chimney towers. In the morning they will be found & their souls will be prayed for. Under cloud feather pillows.

They knew not of mortar. Miller, what are we chasing? We chase ourselves in circles through a town which climbs towards the clouds. & it will not stop there. & we will have to. I saw them run circuits & pictured a tall child throwing sunflower petals that evaporated before they hit the ground. This feeling cynical, then Acacia leaned

her head in her hands, you will see
this through. Hector & The Miller
returned to the willow where they
drunk gin until it blinded them & smoked
woodbines until they could not move.

s c a b s

I

The first boat of immigrants came licking dirty lips on a calm day. It was night. Fuchsia met with scarlet & clouds cowered.

Olive drab took notes while Paris shook thin hands.

Oh how Acacia wept.
The moon refused to show itself.

Desert tan men watched through windows suspicious. The Moon & Earth were empty. Barman Ambrose winds out candles & sits beneath a beer tap. A fence of pine around each red brick house now, well-pruned greenery eyeing the new arrivals like sweating pigs. They sleep in cyan tents for the now. Speaking in torrents, tongues, plots, wealth. They vow to keep to their ways, their own ways; painted faces, wooden entertainments. Boys from the red brick houses slip outside with candles, headed towards the town of tents. Mothers

catch them at the Moon & Earth, with heavy hands flames to smoke go.

s c a b s

I I

The Miller sits alone with ink & paper.
He vows to **write the rise**; every detail
of the town's growth shall be penned
beneath his eyes. In his eyes, with his
hands. Mother claims nonsense & claps

at the slaves. **Wealth son**, a
thing you shall never know. She tugs
at his fingers until he spins thread. The
Miller weaves a net around the cottage
& checks his traps. **Traps to howl the
hounds** around the walls of civilization,
let them come mother says, let them
sleep happy. Fingers will grow into the
circles of history.

s c a b s

I I I

Anoushka & Isidor light candles inside their tent. The yellow fire burns rings of color into the magenta fabric; there is a scene of biblical brightness unfolding.

A lamb is born. It stumbles & struggles with the colors beyond womb-black vegetation; pine green, sap green, moss green, teal. These are new lands my love & we shall be dirt in their palms until gold is heaved from below the earth in vats as big as the ship we came on.

She holds herself with brittle arms & whispers low prayers. These prayers are verses which my grandmother's mother spun into headscarves & wandered fields feeling. Feeling the scythe thread reed & sedge. Isidor, cups of mint tea made with bare

flames. The soil pressed into the fold
of our hands. We held them together
Anoushka, we watched them spray
chemicals & ride machines, you said; let
us ride the machines to red brick homes.
Look at where we are. Twist your neck
to the torn fabric.

 Two rocks in a well of broken birds.

s c a b s

I V

The charioteer sleeps with his head on the body of his wife. **He holds her hand tight white.** The sycamore folds in smoke, black leaves; charred trunk. Dreams, hector says.

Hector

Her?

She died last spring. **Felt her turn blue beside me.** Ran circles in the forest then came back. Still something lingering in her. I saw it. Papercuts, she has papercuts.

Then?

She used to be an ocean in my palms. A vermillion sun lit her from above & she would glow with

the warmth of a fistful of flares. Before
we had smelt the gas she would smell
thyme from the bows of a great oak.
We would fall from its branches, drunk
with wine, & stare as a merciful God
unfolded the plum sky like a blanket
over our bodies. Rye tickled my ears as
she slept with her head in my hands.

They were silent porcelain nights in the old world & I miss
them as I do our youth.

The chariot?
No use now for a long net. There is
nothing. People sleep dreamless.

s c a b s

V

Olive drab makes the desert tan army
haul his throne up to the cathedral tower.
He watches the town & drinks cinnamon.

We must have order, we must have lines. His office mahogany warms eager eyes, this now mine.

The warmth of a stone tower & tall fire;
tents begin to collapse.
Anoushka & Isidor wrap themselves in
the failed canvas of their magenta home.
Pray, Isidor whispers.

Olive drab orders the mines be sunk

& calls for motors to sink them. Oil,
he cries. Maps are drawn of red brick
streets. Workers summoned from tents,
back into the cold spotlights of bleached
women watching from windows.

You will protect, olive drab begins, the

town. You will, with blades, keep
the people in lines & help lower
loads in the port. You shall work
the people as they should be
worked. You may, should you wish,
smile at their sunburnt spines. You
are to watch the mines with keen
eyes; the brutes will hide our gold
in their cheeks should we leave
them with pockets. Pay them in
red bricks & potato. You must be
quick to cut the hands that wander.
Call them by numbers. Invent the
numbers. Change the numbers.

Paris coughs.
You may sit with me, olive drab says.

The desert tan army leaves in riot. They
shout coarse plans & the governor
smiles.

Smile at the flesh of your feet.

s c a b s

VI

Marsha watches the shadows thrown by muscular tree boughs. She rakes her fingers through wet soil & smiles at the dirt. Dirt as the start & end of everything, she thinks. Pounding fists into the earth to re-enter play; the cycle. The human condition is standing back from circles of mindless vegetation, flesh, rot, water, soil.

I am inside an iron loop of vaginas & caskets.
The fortified nature of thought.

s c a b s

VII

The mine sunk, motors making black noise with coal, desert tan moon over frail men.

There are ladders bound with twine & men working for their wives. Your lives in the great cracks of stone which should keep beneath feet; search for anything small enough to be put inside of a ring. The callous laughter of desert tan filters down through the shafts & into blistered ears.

Migrant workers pick rocks, town men build red brick houses, desert tans find paths to walk. A clockwork economy. Isidor throws the weight of his body into an axe. Throws for his wife & red bricks. They hear shudder, the pause of a great mine. Torches inside cold eyes shine on the body of a collapsed man. Isidor reaches out, great arms envelop the fallen miner. He is carried back to the town.

The first casualty of industrial civilization.

Olive drab sighs & falls to sleep.

A wife pounds her husband's stilled heart in blackout rage, alone in a new age; she shouts for a ship to take her back before red brick. She sings for wood & mud.

Isidor

Do I remember life before this?
No

Really, nothing?
No, I came here for the gold.

Work?

It breaks the both of us. I can hold my ribs so that they appear whole, she lets snap against the earth of our tent. Plunge my hands inside of her & prop her body up, I try but she'd have me stop. I come back coal tired with enough gold for one potato. Give it to her, I ate mine on the way. Soon my body will collapse. Nobody will notice. Fuel for the motors & fire for the miners. She is a dying truth.

On the fire?

Yes, it is wild. We are black. They run.

s c a b s

V I I I

Acacia sees the men sent down shafts.
She drinks the liquid gold & trains her
shotgun at desert tan trees, laughing
insane & fitful, fearful & proud. She
is proud to be an island. You do not need
diamond to tug life from rows of soil.
Marsha has left. Fire a summons into the
sand of their beach. Call them back
to thought. Light in the cathedral
tower now. A hunched silhouette
passing past its high window. The
screams of motors from mines. Acacia
dines on stewed vegetables, sitting in a
bowl of sand; she watches them forget their own.

scabs

IX

The Miller writes of sooty migrants,
severe roads & wandering desert tan.
He swallows wide mouthfuls of gin &
water between each sentence, perverse
rebellion against the town's new
found wealth. Wealth in gold & silver
& gemstone. We were wealthy,
he writes, wealth in co-operation &
classlessness.

His mother howls for his ink;
the writings of a madman!
Stand on a family bible & repeat your
heresy.

Averse to the beauty of civilization, she
says. She claps when the boats
arrive. Wetting cracked lips in delight.

He writes again, dreams are steel cages

or glass boxes or straight paths; I am
glad to have slept with hands over ears
on the night of industrial civilization.

scabs

X

It is winter, the colors are all wrong. A sky of dirty nameless hues.

A bleach blonde woman walks back from The Moon & Earth, back to the house with the work-weary husband; sleeping in need of small arms. He waits in dream for her body, sharp rose flesh & narrow stream of breath to curl behind him, but it does not come.

Fifteen steps from the inn she is seized. She is seized by greasy hands & thin wrists, pulled into an alleyway & thrown to the floor. Looking up at a grinning desert tan figure. Screaming half-hearts at the pathetic red-eyes bulging into her body. She feels dreams of industrial civilization collapse, oh vile

minutes. Pale legs & gritted teeth; he
works. A pulsing man, a weak man. His
yellow teeth blow nicotine kisses onto
her neck. He tenses, he sighs & he runs.

Desert tan fades into dark winter.

She cries & throws herself at the red
brick walls of the alleyway. Inside of a

red brick tunnel; a pipedream.
Firing tobacco, all inside the red brick
tunnel must light the brown weed now
as consolation. Maintain well-being with
bad health. Let the desert tan queue
form before your body, for that is all it is;

body. Drink the blood & eat the body.
Let the cathedral die.

j u s t i c e

I

Hector & The Miller sit inside the winter on the roots of the willow. They sip mint tea spiced with whisky & watch the dreamless town, the moths on the roofs, the light in the tower.
There is **no room for dream** in their gold minds now, The Miller says.
I am told the young girl left to find the root of those dreams.
The root of those dreams is **olive drab**.
Olive drab is but **the means for the dreams**.
The desert tan army the means for his dream.
His dream the box for theirs.

They watch the deep ochre sky become

coal & settle. The light in the tower still
shines. This orchestra so foul & drunk.
Candles on every surface. Their breath is
made smoke in the cold air before them.
A dream falls past & Hector knocks
it from the air with quick fists. They
watch the moths flinch in unison.

The Miller laughs & the charioteer
laughs & there is industrial civilization.

j u s t i c e

I I

Marsha rests on the forest floor. She
drifts between sleep & dreams of song.
A black bear lies beside her, fetal & feeble.

The bear is hungry, it wants for acorns &
another bear & a hole in the cliff. It does
not want for motors or silver or towers
or entrance through an alleyway.

She feels closer to the bear than
the town of unrelenting hysteria.
She feels the bear; more human than the
humans in their red brick houses.

She lies with the bear until morning. A
teal morning on the forest floor. Beauty
in the bright merger of green & yellow
against dark bark trunks. The bear leads
her to a clear glass river, lit through with
slow viridian flashes. He catches fish

with his paws & lays them at her feet.
She smiles at the both of them; **there,
then**. Marsha, it is casting their heads
over the horizon that has done this.

j u s t i c e

I I I

The Hotelier wakes in the night to a bruised wife. **She cries over his heart** while he feels veins rise from thick arms. Drawing details he leaves the woman beneath his sheets & sets for the tower. Olive drab is not sleeping,

he cannot sleep, not with such **wild dreams of wealth unfolding** around him. His tobacco burns blue inside his smile, a crescent of dry lust.
Yes? He asks the Hotelier.
My wife, your men….
They are but men, let them be.

Let them be?
The Hotelier throws a glass vase to the floor & lapses into hysterical laughter.
Let them be?
A fist launched at the face of olive drab, his high cheek bruising almost instantly.

So thin the skin of power, so thick the arms of its children. He sends four quick hits into the floorboards & four desert tan men drag the Hotelier away.

Olive drab writes the night through & when the gray morning arrives he stares from his window at a new, just world.

The Wife

The red bricks?
They are fences. They are fences & guiding ropes. Would you like to see my burns? Hold my hands & spill the water. My palms are empty, what am I to do?

The man?
My man. He has left. Gone for to find olive drab & beat justice into him. We will see it in the morning. I am sure I will be forgiven for this. Am I beautiful? Am I the most

beautiful?

A last meal?
Gold. Break my teeth to grit, I will swallow. We can play in the shallows as children. We can draw years. Please lead me away.

Castle?
You see the land spread & from where? Prophecy, she lies unbound. We can bring her into being.

Others?
I watch no one. Sit inside this box & watch my feet. I care little for the dirty workers washing themselves with urine. They ought to know melting flesh. I will for them to sleep on torture racks. I still feel him inside of me.

j u s t i c e

I V

Acacia writhes in wet sheets.

Outside it rains, winter rain.
The drum of water a soft canvas for the
sporadic cries of motors from the island.
She watches the island pass a night in
smoke, by morning the smoke has not
cleared & she has not slept. Drinking
liquid gold from the well she prays
on her beach. Forehead buried in soft
sand, toes curled, eyes streaming. White
waves break over her desperate skull.
On the island's beach a worker points
her out to a desert tan, who smiles
inside of his fantasy.

She stares back unaware.

I call for Marsha & the motors play rape.
Virtuoso.

j u s t i c e

V

The charioteer runs horses down to the town but they will not take the roads & he is forced to leave them. He marvels at the mathematical asphalt rivers & dead terraced houses. The port is a wide gray claw now. The town enveloped in a thick smoke. The Moon & Earth is desert tan. The sweat of migrants laced with gold in iron crates bound for the oceans. He watches all of this & says,

this is not us.

j u s t i c e

V I

Olive drab calls for **assembly** inside the Cathedral.
The bishops too are sent to pews while the town files in.

Hector & The Miller sit awkwardly at the back, cigarettes in their hands. They sit with the migrants, in front of them the workers & in front of them desert tan. The desert tan army sits with crossed arms & wide smiles. The migrants curl against each other.

Olive drab stands before them & I feel the migrants holding the hearts of their loved ones.

He smiles.

He raises his arms.

Two men carry out the Hotelier, tied to his wife, both cut & caked in dried islands of blood. They are gagged, eyes screaming, & placed on the floor.

JUSTICE, olive drab says, what we need is justice. Allowing for motiveless acts of violence would sow a seed that would draw the carpet from underneath this society, from under us all. There is only one way to keep safe the earth from such seeds, he says, nodding at the two men stood beside him. They lift the Hotelier & his wife once more & lead the town from the cathedral to the east cliff. Migrants return to tents. Bleached women, workers, & desert tan watch with a novel closeness the fate of one man & his wife.

The slow sinking of two bodies below the cliff's edge.

Four eyes still unprepared for the end, even as they meet it.

A bleach blonde woman lets out a cry &
she is struck by her muscled husband.

She flees the scene into the forest.

.

h y m n s

I

Hector leaves the cathedral for his willow.
His heart races a slow body, feet
drag the rotting leaves & shaking fingers
cradle an aching head. Rain clears to
leave black mist born of filth from motors.
Migrants mine without sleep to keep
themselves in potato. He meets a frail
blonde woman on the roots of his willow,
she talks in webs of her husband &
his heavy hands. He holds her until her
scarlet eyes will hold to his. They sip
ginseng tea taken from the ships by The
Miller & watch the town. Olive drab is
addressing those who remain on the
cliff. She sleeps in his lap that night. The
Miller lays a woolsack over the both
of them. He sits beside Hector while
Clementine sleeps. Drinks himself weary.
& what now? Hector says.
We sleep.

h y m n s

I I

While Marsha sleeps beside the river
a bear falls into her companion. He
presents her with fish & she leads him
to a cave. Marsha wakes alone &
starts for the field of the root of dreams
of industrial civilization.

Snow begins to fall.

h y m n s

I I I

Hector, Clementine, & The Miller wake
in snow. They shake it from their hair
& Hector makes ginseng tea over a fire
inside the willow. Clementine holds to
him & pulls out **promises of a new
home.**

The migrants wake to another day
inside the colossal hole. They strip
down to bare chests & launch their axes
at the stone walls, calling for **gold &
potato**. The workers beat shoes, pots,
ships, & gold into shapes for olive drab.
He watches them & says, **this is
good.** The husband of Clementine
takes a new wife & works unloading
ships at the port.

Months pass in black smoke waves

while white noise bellows from the mine
motors.

They have justice, gold &
red brick.

p o p p i e s

I

The migrants tear branches from forest trees to hold up their torn cyan tents. Some snap & **reach for food from the pockets** of desert tan, they are thrown then into the gold bearing ocean & replaced.

The spring comes & migrants rot with disease. They arrange tents in towns & sit with each other in warmth. Isidor cradles Anoushka & lays kisses on her eyes as she sleeps.

Lines are drawn between the layers **coal & gold**, sleep in **rock & on velvet.**

She prays & cries inside of a wooden crate, one thousand miles from the town; it falls to the ocean floor & splits open. Her body bends in the ersatz tent. Isidor lights **all the candles he can steal** but still she sleeps with wet eyes.

Anoushka

Crow?

Oh you may watch my eyes but **I will anger**. Quick to anger & spit, rage with small fists against a wide chest. I care not for odds. Will I die throwing? You think I care for him? **I care for my body & my mind.** Pretty immigrants clinging to each other? I am firing the stacks. I am a thousand miles from here. **I feel nothing of them.** I know nothing. I cannot hear or touch or see or feel **their violence, their sadness, their will** to sit beside others. Maroon like the women who cry for their husbands' bleeding knuckles. What could he think of me? What may he know? Perhaps I will to right myself in amongst the shards of red glass. I see nothing of this. I understand none. I have hands & I have eyes, sadness? Violence? I have them nothing. Let him mine the gold & leave me his meager earnings. I feel nothing.

You can break the bones of my legs, I do not walk. Plunge into my skull with laughter. This is it, all of it. They say we are to die here. They say we are to end.

Words carry greed carry hearts & lives & us, this, men.

p o p p i e s

II

In April the first ship of Opium arrives. Olive drab smokes in his tower, his eyes light & the town turns. In The Moon & Earth desert tan men & workers raise tall glasses to industrial civilization, a thanks for the wealth that has fallen into their palms. They sink vodka from the ships & pinch their women with drunken hands.

I see them spin their hearts upon the tables.

p o p p i e s

I I I

Marsha finds a red brick ruin beside one great oak. She sits inside the three low walls & holds her knees, her eyes against the bone. **Prophecy** howled by the wind wraps scarves around her pale neck. She beats **warnings** into the bricks & sparrows sit upon her shoulders. **They crow prayers** into her ears, scratching at her flesh with their claws. She feeds them with fistfuls of snow. **A match is struck**; they reach out with cracked beaks & singe black feathers, which curl cold into the day. As the sun sits above her head, now is stretched into white puddles of dirt & ice. She sleeps inside the ruin for three days. The sparrows scatter leaves over her body & devour her hair.

p o p p i e s

I V

Paris is called to the tower.
Inside he meets the wild eyes of olive
drab with a bow.
There is something you need do, he says.
Paris nods.
Glass boxes will be arriving on the next
ship, put the moths inside them & stack
them in the red brick square.
Why keep them alive at all?

They make our lives richer,
creatures, they lend us color.

Color, Paris echoes.
When the glass boxes arrive, Paris
gathers the moths from roofs using long
nets. He cages them.
The boxes are left in the square & lit
from above with candles.

Paris

Orders?
He made me take the moths. Put
them inside the boxes, he said. I did it
of course. I believe, we all do. This
tunnel will burn out the better.
Sky the side through will be angel blue,
fuchsia will be a bad memory.

Gold?
Watch it, sell it, send it the oceans
over. We are but men. What can we do?

Concrete?
Beauty in the lines of buildings. They
bind everything into motive &
work.

shou sui

I

Marsha reaches the field in morning. Watching avarice play with dogs amongst the poppies. She is a young girl with wild ginger hair, inside of a simple white dress. She laughs & sketches motors onto a slice of yew bark. Guilt tripping over blue cheeks.

Avarice?
I only wanted motors.
Motors bring poor men, bring moth boxes, bring black.
I only wanted gold.
& what use is metal?
Mother would lay it on my breast & cry beauty. Do you think I am beautiful?
Your dogs are restless.

Am I beauty?
They are blind.

I am going to throw myself into
formaldehyde & die beautiful.
Snow.
Yes, it burns my hands.
The girl's hair falls from her & her eyes move apart.
You are an ugly little girl!
She laughs.

Motor, motor, motor!
Rrrrrrrrrrrrrrrrrrrrrrrrrrrrrr rrrrm!

Faster, Faster!

The dogs circle Marsha, she sits in the rotting sedge & lights a cigarette.
Apologies, avarice says, picking up her hair. Would you like tea? Marsha does not answer & the sky splits into white fragments while the girl boils a kettle.
She returns with ginseng tea & sits.
I'm sorry, I just wanted to hear a motor.
Motor fuel can stain hearts. Draw potato.
I drew potato for a thousand years.
The girl leads her to a hole wider than

the cathedral, filled with the charred remains of paper. Sparrows in the trench scratch at faint shapes.
Today I drew little red flowers & forgot to say prayers.
The girl leads her to a small wooden chest filled with black & white sketches of poppies.

Will you draw these onto me?

The girl passes her a small bottle of red india ink & Marsha drinks it, feeling her heart glow against the bitter cold.

Addiction makes faint the heart.
Am I a good little girl?

You are the most beautiful cage on this island.

Will you show me your heart?

Marsha proffers her wet heart slowly, the girl traces the passage of thought through veins & arteries with a small finger. She smiles.
Would you like to see my heart?
Yes.

THEN I WILL SHOW YOU MY PALMS! The girl says, laughing & throwing a fast slap.
I don't believe in industrial civilization.
I am the most beautiful stone in the moth box.
The girl leads her to a great redwood, hung over with sketches of motors tied with yellow string. The sun bores rough holes in high papers. A small girl holds to red bark.
You are to fell the redwood.
Avarice laughs.
Here, the girl says, placing a moth on Marsha's shaking hands, the last dream.

Avarice

Now?
Play, will you play with me? In the town he lays my roads. He is silent. I wanted olive drab hands to comb my

hair & hold me to the trees but they
were burned bright by gold.

Me?
Only for the hoarse shout of motors.
Never for men in mines, justice or
concrete. I have pure dreams
& they have fists.

Lines for the maps?
Take it down. All of it. Still I sit sorry
for wild dreams, they will to dine on
gold; tearing the land. Am I beautiful?
Did you ever see such
beauty?

Time?
I can feel it in my roots & it cries.

s h o u   s u i

I I

Hector sows seeds while Clementine blows on a woodbine in the bough of his sycamore. The Miller making clothes for the three of them while his mother screams incendiary from her bed in the backroom. Lanterns are strung the town over. Small holes in the sun's skin. Green glass bottles of gin line circles around the tree. The night comes slow & hot; Olive drab smoking opium in his tower of motor oil,

Desert tan men drinking hell in The Moon & Earth,

Workers holding to wives & children in red brick homes,

Migrants smiling dirty in vodka fits,

Acacia tasting sand & brine in a beach sprint with the moon,

Paris waiting impatient at the dock,

Marsha sleeping in the ruin with the last dream,
Hector, Clementine, & The Miller dizzy with false dream inside the willow,

This is how the new year passes. Shou Sui.

shou sui

III

The new year comes with saffron
sun over the sleeping town. The sea

is a wild blend of water & steel, a

thoughtless storm of revelry.
It will be months, Paris says, stood on
the cliff beside olive drab.
The solemn leader looks pensive,
scratching furiously at his thin arms.

All ships bound for port have been raped
with dry saltwater & forced to the ocean
floor. One year will pass before the
ocean pulls up its sweat wet trousers &
leaves the dark alleyway.

What now, Clementine whispers in the
willow,
resource substitution, Hector mouths.

Clementine

Them?
They took me. He held me while they rolled out the **rotting carpet of justice**. Making pots of ginseng tea, passing tree smoke against the solemn winter. We have good days in the tree, while they work themselves into holes for gold. **I sow seeds & we dine happy.**

The town?
It will break all of this, I am not sure what we can do.

shou sui

IV

Olive drabs calls assembly in the cathedral. Spit showers announce the storm; no coal for the motors, what can we do?

Wood!

The forest shall be felled, the wood will fire our motors & the land will bear poppies. Thousands of beautiful poppies. Poppies bloom & die beneath my skin. Tug at the optic nerves until my eyes fall down my throat. I have a scarlet lust inside of my reach. Thread poppy chains through my veins & work my flesh. Red beauty. Beautiful red pouring through cracks in the steam of this sauna. Steam soaked body content in a

field of poppies with a thousand wild
dogs pawing at my eyes & at my ears &
at my mouth & throat & hands & heart.

saints

PREMISE THREE:

Our way of living – industrial civilization – is based on, requires, & would collapse very quickly without persistent & widespread violence.

Endgame Vol. 1, The Problem of Civilization : Derrick Jensen

The Miller

I ran for hiding beneath the house, the orphans were sent to sea. I clawed at mud with shaped steel until a hole rose from the ground. I fell. The room cavernous, stone & silk. Candles in the corners threw white light over the tapestries; men, beasts, gold, & oceans.

Three sat in the corner, smoking & laughing; Michael, Margaret, & Catherine; Saints.

h u n g e r

I

Acacia did nothing when the desert
tan came. She watched their small boat
grow clear through the haze of rain
on the sea & made angels in the sand
while they lowered themselves into her
well of liquid gold. More men came.

Men with motors. Soon her island
hummed like the other. The men drank
themselves wild & watched the moon
bounce its white hands off the liquid
gold. Their eyes watered red while the
morning came.

The sun was shy & the men slept with it on their
backs.

hunger

II

Marsha stalked the bears through mountains. Miles fell behind her red eyes & soft footfalls as she traced their paths. She crouched beside the mouth of their cave. The night fell scarlet around her, clouds drew together & made a solemn temple in the sky. Gates opened & a thousand sparrows made quick their escape. The bears slept happy, cradling each other's bodies against the insanity of the town. She crept in & slit their throats with a rock from the floor. Their heads were slowly removed & she climbed into the body of the bear.

Marsha slept wet with tears & blood inside the bear.

h u n g e r

I I I

He took us down beneath the mill & we stood beside them.
Michael was the first to stand, he spoke with quick determination, deep & proud.

Floods will draw your town.
We can do nothing.
You must.
Nothing.
Fire them! Catherine screamed.
The Miller sat.
Olive drab holds fast his tower.
Then we knock it from beneath him.
The land will still be **concrete, hole & opium.**
You would have us drink the weeds?

Burn the roots!
Smell the jasmine & forget it all.
You are saints!
You are men.

Will you watch steel dreams break weak minds?
Oh the wine.
Margaret sways, the green glass bottle of her hands falls to pieces beside her feet.
She sleeps, laughs Michael.

Throw avarice from the cliffs.
She is a girl, she knows nothing.
Humming motor noise in a field of poppies.
She has dogs.
I have dogs, they scar my ankles.
Your eyes are opening.

QUIET Michael pleads.
The hair slips from Catherine's white face. Her eyes wide red.

You are an ugly saint!

Go, go, go!
Grow & fire!
Make wild the men inside their pits!
Mmmmmmmmmmm-mmmmmmmmmmmmm-mmm!

Michael places her fallen hair back upon her head.

Sorry, she mumbles.

The saints sleep silent beneath The Miller's house. A thick, dirty sleep cast by discovery of the claret wine of civilization.

hunger

IV

A desert tan man laid coarse oil hands upon Acacia's thighs. She hit him with a stone & he died.

h u n g e r

V

Isidor lit a candle & Anoushka spat it black. He tried to hold her but she cried & flailed.
Why!
For you.
I want to die with gold skin.
You wanted sun.
This is sun?
Prophecy comes clothed.
Your mouth is open.
Please watch the candles.
You think these flames make do for a lost sun?
The sun will burn out.
Light.
You wanted light.
We could have burned our hair.

He sits beside the road. Existence pulsing like a lung. He sits inside. Talk of belief when the chariot passes. You put your feet as: here, here, here, or you will die, this is the only stipulation. I am not God but you must will to live to live this well. & if *beauty did so lie in fields of desolation, we would be made men &* the sun would be at our heels. *She would chase us as we chase bones, as dogs follow tails or as gold follows eyes. See that we are to die in mines*

left to grow into great lakes & swallow us. *Swallowed whole by the cage of cold. Lick ice metal & make sharp your brain. Do well.*

Son, we never left the bridge in the birdcage. You heard the swallow crow & clubbed it to soft death. Do you hold everything I collected?

I collected the ocean & poured it down your throat.

He is holding his breath & feeling his body.

Waiting to forget the body, the eyes, the ears. Not wanting to love but be free. Outside of the bent lines, space & time enveloping ALL. Not all, the souls of the truly free smile from beyond structure. Count breaths & forget feeling. Feeling made her claw the walls & fill the ashtray. She could do without us all. She could eat only stars & sleep only when the sky had been emptied. Her horizons had always sat beyond my fingers. We are beautiful.

She was beauty, that summer.

I have believed for years in things that were not mine to believe in. Each action will face a bastard backlash, she said. There was an eastern sun, disinclined to pull at her collar. I had prayed for tradition to allow us our clothes.

I had not eaten for months. My ribs were toys for the rich. We dined on nails from

our hands & feet, you tried to steal a horse.
Still feeling things, still sitting trapped.
When time should see fit to draw its own
lines, I shall cup your breasts.

We can grow trees, grind paper, & write our
bodies away. Should I write the heart, the
head & the hands, then there will be nothing
left for me to carry. My spine is shot through
*with **the lead of being**. My hands can*
clap but not carry. Beauty emanates absurd
violence. The fragmentation of concrete over
*bare skin. **Is this beauty now?** When I*
sit naked & denounce physical sensation, is
that beauty? Your pride will eat your beauty,
it will kiss hers. Drag her through the streets
on your shoulders. Watch their eyes taste
your pride but hold back her beauty. Read
the angels nothing.

There is some slight taint that breeds a green
cancer inside of me. I tried to remove it with
a yew bough & then I slept.

h e a r t

I

The yellow morning & Clementine crept
into the hole. She met with Catherine
while the other saints lay sleeping.
I want these mornings as circles.
You wish for trees?
Hold the colors in your palms.
I feel the fuchsia drink your town.
Inside of my eyes.
I see them shot through with bricks &
gold.
You feel the metal cut throat?
Blessed are those who lie in ditches.
Hector sings of days before civilization.
Tell him all days are these days.
Oh but he will fall.
Let all men fall.
You are a saint!
I see,

Blessed are those who sink to their knees.
Show me your heart?
I can show you only palms & eyes.
Your eyes whisper water.

THE FLOODS!
You pray prophecy?

THE FLOODS! THE TOWN!
Sit with me.
Clementine passes a cigarette to the riled saint. They smoke quietly while morning filters down the hole.
Sit against the floods.

Spines will shatter.
You are too long shattered, built from olive drab glass; be patient.
I will lead wild dogs into the glass & they will **bleed us safe**.
Catherine falls into loud laughter.

You think the flesh of dogs

will save you?
My fingers are so thin, you see them?
Perhaps the flesh of wild dogs will bear your weight.

I will drown godly.

Blessed be those who die with golden stacks.

Truly, the kingdom of heaven wants for gold?

We all want for gold.

I want for the dogs & the floods & the girl from the field.

You are young.

You are a wild-tongued saint.

I am not a saint.

h e a r t

II

Clementine sat with the sun as a
morning came of age. The saints woke
with heavy heads & talked defense
while they smoked woodbines in their
room beneath the mill.

h e a r t

I I I

Olive drab leads miners to the woods.
They land redwoods with fast axe
swings & sing **work, sweat, wood**
beneath the fuchsia sky.

Trees rise in stacks the height of red
brick houses.

Hector cries.
The Miller hides his eyes.
Clementine buries her face into sand on
the beach.

Fire the last, olive drab screams.
The last trees go up yellow,
shivers in the tangerine afternoon. They
run from the forest; the Lunatic, the wild
dogs & little avarice, tripping herself in
short steps. Hector leads them to the

room beneath the mill, the saints cry, drink claret, & fall asleep beside each other. On the floor an inch of brine.

The Saints woke, watched the town, then drank themselves back to sleep.

Hector & St. Michael smoked opium & tried to eat each other. They slept for three days.

Clementine ate sand until St. Catherine beat her, yellow rings.

St. Margaret swallowed her rosary & killed the dogs.

h e a r t

I V

Isidor held that light was theirs & they may run with it.

Anoushka shouted LIES.
She walked on the beach & broke the wing of a sparrow with stone tied to potato. You will live, she told the spinning bird.

l i g h t s

I

The Lunatic beats the walls of the room beneath the mill. He calls for saints with fire, oil, eyes. Wide eyes, he says. Eyes like a witch, watching her own feet curl in the thrall of flame.

lights

II

Avarice met with the Lunatic on the
beach. It was morning gray & scarlet. He
sat cross-legged while she placed her
small head into his lap.
The ocean for us, she says.
Take it in your eyes.
Beneath my dress, she replies laughing.

You are the most beautiful.

Please present my skull with jewels in
the eyesockets.
There shall be opals.

Keep me clean of gold & coal.

I will keep you clean of chimney smoke.
The thick smoke beats my lungs.
Your brain is in my legs.
My thoughts & your bones.
Sand.

Do you promise to meet me on the ocean floor when the town has gone?

I will meet you with the sun.

She shall dine with us.
We will sleep on glass.
Sew my lips & I will feed yours.

We will be happy.

Smoke beneath the water.
The saints?

We shall drown the saints!

They came from beneath the mill.
They are but The Miller's children.

The Miller's eyes are white & wild.

He is a desert tan!

We should drown him too.
We should drown all of this.

Yes, they rape dry the forest.

We will rape their sad little bodies until the sun sinks.

& the sun shall sink into us!

We will burn.

Burn happy.
Your eyes are failing.
Catherine says Jesus will save me.
Jesus sits on the sun & watches them kill everything.

They kill the sky.

lights

III

Autumn came with rains & the sea crept into the room beneath the mill. It washed sobriety into the eyes of the Saints & Michael woke them all with his plan:

WE ARE BLEEDING INTO THE BRICKS OF THIS TOWN. Concrete is a vice but we are Saints (Catherine coughed). Let us lead these few from here. Promised land, a holy town. There must be something. A guide will manifest, God wills it. We will lead these men from the clutches of the tide of evil, OF INDUSTRIAL CIVILIZATON! We shall save them, salvation. They shall be God's people, free & joyful. Let us promise them grass & trees, for these they shall have. They will be happy

beyond the dreams that hands can claw.
They will see clear glass as far as their
eyes will care to look.

l i g h t s

I V

Acacia wrote a thousand promises into
the beach sand & denied the tides.

l i g h t s

V

Olive drab smokes opium in his tower.
He decorates the floor with soil & laughs
at the floral walls. He calls for a desert
tan soldier. Undress, he says. Olive
drab laughs at the naked man. Take me
to the poppy fields.
The king rides his pet to a plain of thoughts.
He dismounts & runs;
runs through the poppies while they
run through him. He winds them
around his fingers & they crawl
through his nostrils.

His bones scar red, eyes black in
the hole.

lights

VI

The saints sat with Hector, Clementine,
& Avarice on the beach.
We will try, Michael said, & Avarice
pulled at his golden hair.

You will save nothing, she said.
Let me dream your town white.
I dreamt it black; coal is a bitter love.
The waves break white.
Over a black bed of dead fish.

Am I the most beautiful?
You are white as the waves over tower.
Watch the clouds burst.
Show me your hands St. Michael.
Avarice holds his long fingers to her
chest.
You feel my heart?
It beats with dark while men murder in the mines.
They crow pretty hymns from filthy
holes.

Blessed be those who wait for death.
& kiss him like a mother.

l i g h t s

V I I

Clementine & Hector sat beside the
poppy fields, evening. She made chains
as long as the town & wound them
round his neck. Let her die, she said.
He thought of his wife & put palms
to ears. A sparrow landed beside her,
cigarette in its beak. Let her die, she
said. The sparrow wished for trees.
Gunpowder made citrus explosions in
the sky & the Lunatic stood grinning &
clutching matches on the edge of town.

Let her die, she said. He launched
powders into the air until it held more
color than the ground. Olive drab
laughed himself to his knees. Let her die,
she said.

Hector whispered that they could not marry, for
the Saints would not allow it.

sun

I

Olive drab stood with the roof of his tower & shouted himself hoarse: we take ourselves RICHES, steal; for yourself RUN RUN RUN & cry within thin walls. These things, hold them & **burn everything**. Your wives are pretty but watch my eyes, for the seas will swell & swallow our bodies whole. Bones will break **yellow, sinew, blood, muscle, torrents!** You are ready for nothing. PLAY THE POPPY. Men fell yourselves in fields. Scythe limbs from your fickle bodies. Hold to stone & clutch at the tides. Will the moon rape purple fields? I will it, LET IT BE. He lights a long opium pipe. Drag them behind the horses! Let the charioteer play vile games with your flesh. We will all be happy. The tower is falling. Watch me eat your hearts. Let us play ourselves! I will

win! Skin me gold, make wide this smile & yellow these eyes. There is beauty inside you, turn your hearts out on your precious crops & sing your hymns into the earth. SHE WILL LISTEN! She will cry with you. Who prayed floods? THEY WILL COME! Let

us wait with each other until gold gold god copper. You manned the ship! I know this. You. Pretty waves

eat matches. Let us light bonfires & fall into them. I will watch you now, you may RUN.

s u n

I I

I saw him scratching at himself, blood rising to fill the exposed spaces in his skin. He cries & smokes. He shouts lunacy. I do not want gold. He can have the gold, each sharp stone. He can swallow them, smoke them, sell them, & buy love. They say he has lost his eyes in the poppy fields. His clumsy feet will crush them to nothing. I collect nothing now, I keep it with my broken glass. My teeth are beautiful. Bite myself back, hands up; white scarves & dried poppies.

sun

III

The saints sit beside Hector's willow.
They smoke heavy woodbines & blow
smoke into each other's faces. Sun falling
slow, night brittle cold.
I want for gold, Catherine says.
Your bones will stain yellow.
Is this town ours?
This town is his.
Does he hold the birds?
He crushes them, Catherine says
in laughter.
They watch the town pulse orderless.
I can't dream, Michael says.
Place bullion beneath your skull.
Dirt in the dream.
Sleep in the poppies.
I would rather sleep in my own skin.
Salt your skin with water from the ocean.
Jesus is angry.

It's just night.
Michael takes Catherine's hand, takes Margaret's hand, takes Michael's.
Can we lead them someplace else?
They would rather sleep with bullion.

Gold is a sad lover.
Small hands.
The Miller watches you, Michael tells Catherine.

He looks for gold inside of me.
The gold is in the trees.
We can sit in the trees.
Trees burn.

Skin them!
The Miller will marry me happy.
Is this the time for marriage?

This is the time for everything.
Are we setting fires?
They have been set.

men

The ocean bursts once more into a
melancholy frenzy of granite waves.
Gray clouds melted into the ocean & the
ocean melted into the beach. Avarice &
Acacia were watching each other when

it came. RUN, Acacia shouted. They
threw their bodies into the water &
dragged themselves through the ocean.
Rain beat holes into the waves. They met
in the ocean. Held to each other.

THEY COME FOR THE GOLD.
MOTORS.
I WILL WARM YOUR HEART.

They swam together back to Acacia's
island.

lessons

I

Olive drab stood before an empty
cathedral. The pews stood scarred
where the orphans had scratched
names into them with black fingernails.
He watched smugly the complacent
audience. The complacent audience
itched, awkward. The sky made itself
known through wide tears in the ceiling.
He felt content: Raise your heads, your
arms must be weary. **We have made
ground.** See that **the ground is
beauty**, see that the beauty is jewel
laced & whole. Not a man could crack
our progress now. OH & OUR HOUSES,
statues at the end of the path we have
cut, **they shine**. We are clean as the
mind of Jesus. White skin & pulsing blue
veins. We are alive, **this is success.**
Now your lips know it: we are clear. Do

you feel clear? We could swim for years now. Poppies & timber. Burn the fuel to warm your blood. Everything we feel now is progress. There are still flies but they lay oppressed in pools of dew. We are untouchable. This island is ours. Boats & bricks.

l e s s o n s

I I

Isidor cried & Anoushka bit her lip for the blood that would fall.
I felt the sun, she said.
Sun.
The sun is running & we have lost our legs.

Your idle mind has made you wild!
Hold me.
You want to sleep in light.
You are light.
We hid on the ships.
Remember father Yan?
His voice sculpting the good book.
Jesus will come.
There are Saints, they say.
I saw the Saint free the moths.
That night I dreamt every color.

It was a sun?
It was gold.

union

Catherine & The Miller marry on the
cliff. She wears gray cloth. He will later
write that she tarnished the bullion he
had stolen when civilization was young.
St. Catherine felt nothing. She would
later feel that The Miller mattered more
than God's word. They sat in a circle; the
saints, The Miller, Hector, Clementine.
The Lunatic was crying for doors in the town.
Little Avarice & Acacia watched from
their beach. Speeches were made:

Hector
With days so lost as these, everything
we say will be all we have. We must hold
to each other. The floods will come & we
will drown. What can we do but sit
happy?

St. Michael
We came here from a hole; lost as the
kings of your island, & now see us

here. We are all to fall in time but let us crow now. Let us live. Let us be.

Margaret produced wine & all drank. All smiled. All watched the morning begin to rise. Little Avarice wept for the day she knew would come. The ocean played parley with a silver sun.

The Miller
On the first day of gold, when they opened the earth, I stumbled. The skin of my palms began to crack & I fell. Hector drank. The town ran with dreams. The Saints have saved the last days.

St. Catherine

I am a waste of time. He says beauty, I see crimson. When the waters come we will be here.

All sat silently drinking until the Lunatic ran into the circle's center.

The Lunatic

YOU ARE ALL SO BEAUTIFUL! We are going to live forever. Especially Michael. Pretty Michael, Jesus wants to hold you. You have eyes like cattle, beautiful, beautiful cattle. I write prayers for men smaller than you. Make it be!

Michael read verses to the pair & pronounced them wed. Avarice & Acacia cheered & flung liquid gold around themselves. Morning led over the ocean like a naked angel watching stars. The saints sang hymns while wine fell in streams down their chests.

I killed a calf. The golden calf. All sacrifice is good. You left the horse for dead & whispered we are alone. I felt like a dead cherub. You die when you drop your body, escape feeling & forget the flame before your eyes. MY EYES ARE BURNING. Save me.

Wrap my body in silk & carry it through the fire. Can you see the sun? It is pouting & mouthing prayers.

There are prayers written into my head. **Needs**, *they say,* **Wants.**

There is a circle of trees & a wine-fuelled chariot. My face is bulging with wax. I survived. My face is gone. **I am going to leave you.**

We have facial injuries far worse than the scars of gold.

Is your mouth moving? You appear as a quaint manifestation. **I am angry.** *This is anger. I want for human features. I lay sacrifice at all the feet I can find. What for the donor? I will steal identity. These are still feelings.* **I do not want to feel.** *Why do you lay your hands on me mother?* I want to lay in dark.

disease

I

Michael ran wild into the black town. He set free the moths & shouted from the town square: we are free hearts, do not work for bullion. Your houses will burn. Your houses will be crushed by great waves. I feel the ocean swell. Brine will cleanse this festering air. Your lungs are rotting. See the filth in this circle of destruction, please. Pray for plagues to take down these bricks. A band of desert tan men ran at him with knives.

The town laughed inside its smoke sphere while he died.

d i s e a s e

I I

The Saints, Hector, Clementine, & The Miller mourned his death with old nails on the beach. They lined up their hearts along the cliff & kicked them into the sea.

d i s e a s e

III

The Lunatic dripped kerosene trails through the town. He wound around each red brick house & sang prayers to himself. On the beach he threw a match into the trail & howled as the **rings brought down the town**. He watched gold make black. The Saints sat with Hector beside his Sycamore, with woolsacks over their bodies & woodbines in their mouths. They felt the warmth as relief. People in the town filed out of their houses & stood in huddles as their lives burned to nothing.

The Lunatic whispered Michael & cried into the ocean.

Rain began to fall.

They took my heart. You would like to know how to take a heart. You hold the mouth.

*It worked. **I feel nothing.** There are a thousand names for this. I know none. You believe me. **I am beautiful.** Beauty is senseless. There is beauty in rape. I have beautiful hands. You are something to hold & be held by. **We are people.***

floods

PREMISE SEVEN:

The longer we wait for civilization to crash – or the longer we wait before we ourselves bring it down – the messier the crash will be, & the worse things will be for those humans & non-humans who live during it, & for those who come after.

Endgame Vol. 1, The Problem of Civilization : Derrick Jensen

I will sell you poppies pay me in gold I will sell you flesh pay me in oil I will sell you stone pay me in land I will sell you men pay me in spices.

She saw that the floods were coming & she fell to her knees:
Blessed be those who drink their neighbors.
Blessed be those with scars.
Blessed be those who eat the metals.
Blessed be those who sleep with moths in their heads & hands.
Blessed be those who keep blind.
Blessed be those who light fires.
Blessed be those with hardened fists.
Blessed be those who crawl around us.
Blessed be the bleached women, their thoughts & their hearts.

Blessed be those who shoot wild.
Blessed be those who tried to run.
Blessed be those who can count colors.
Blessed be the oil men.
Blessed be those who haul stone.
Blessed be those who came before this.
Blessed be those who will follow.
Blessed be the Saints, the Cattle, & the Crows.
Blessed be the bones inside our skin.
Blessed be the skulls of kings.
Blessed be those who lunge at fear.
Blessed be those who sleep in white.
Blessed be those who eat dirt & drink brine.
Blessed be those who ate

the gas.
Blessed be those who tore eyes in the land.

Blessed be the men that reaped everything.

She felt brine crawl into her ears & she slept.

When the floods came he was smoking inside of the oak. Hector tried to laugh but the water crushed his lungs to bark & he choked. She had said that he would choke &, sure as words, he was dying with a full chest. His eyes threw

light on his heart, they bulged black &
bruised purple, yellow, green; the sky
is painted with the fingers of a drunk
child. The child probes his stomach

in weary jest, it longs for **the cry of motors.** Hector pulls at his ears, he
wants them from his skull before death.
She said that his ears would notice long
before his eyes.
Clementine tried to calm him with her
shaking fingers. She lit their cigarettes

& sung their hymns. It was a night. **It was a night of smoke.** A bonfire
had been lit on the beach. The Saints
cried for Michael & The Miller cried for
Catherine's tears & the Lunatic screamed
& threw rocks.
I found Marsha inside of the bear. The

cave smelt of blood & jasmine. **I held her & wiped the blood from her nose.** Her eyes were
wide.

All of the eyes were wide.

The two saints shouted prophecy
until the purr of the wave drowned out
their calls.
Olive drab smoked. He smoked until the
room fell apart & the wave was silent.
His wife would have killed him. She
died of black plague in a town far from
ships, gold, & opium.
& it was silent then. A thousand
bones broke at once. Bricks fell. The
Lunatic laughed high over the town. I
remember. Planes flew over our heads,
they dropped papers & the papers read:
GET RICH QUICK. The wave
threw bodies. Everything came
down. The Mine was filled & the
black brine was laced with gifts of gold.
A pike ate the gold & everyone bent to
his will.
Sometimes I pretend that we are not
waiting beneath a wave. We left with the

sailors on the first ship. The port came
to us drunk. Drunk but happy. This new
land, you said, this new land is for us. It
was for us. We bought into gold but we
bought in gladly, godly & quiet.
Isidor held Anoushka & sang. She forced
her way into his heart & died with it
open beside her.
Acacia? Avarice? The wave catches
them too. Avarice holds Acacia's hand &
smiles.
I wanted to believe that the Lunatic
would never drown. He kept screaming
FIRE IT OFF ME, I want to believe that
he screamed forever. No one screams
forever, I found that in my wet heart.

I want to get rich quick. Do
you have hands? Then you will reach.

PREMISES TEN & FOURTEEN:

The culture as a whole & most of its members are insane. We are individually & collectively encultured to hate life, hate the natural world, hate the wild, hate animals, hate women, hate children, hate our bodies, hate & fear our emotions, hate ourselves. If we did not hate the world, we could not allow it to be destroyed before our eyes. If we did not hate ourselves, we could not allow our homes – & our bodies – to be poisoned.

Endgame Vol. 1, The Problem of Civilization : Derrick Jensen

Ben Brooks was born in 1992. This is his third novel. He currently lives in Gloucester, England.

WE TAKE ME APART
Molly Gaudry

FIRST YEAR
{ *an mlp anthology* }

AN ISLAND OF FIFTY
Ben Brooks

**WHEN ALL OUR DAYS ARE NUMBERED
MARCHING BANDS WILL FILL THE STREETS &
WE WILL NOT HEAR THEM BECAUSE WE WILL
BE UPSTAIRS IN THE CLOUDS**
Sasha Fletcher

[www.mudlusciouspress.com]